DEVIL YOU DON'T KNOW

Also by Alexandria Blaelock

SHORT STORY COLLECTIONS
The Histories of Hayward Hall
Lovelorn, Lovestruck and Love at First Sight
Common or Garden Variety Heroes
Case Files of the Wilkinson Detective Agency
Unavoidable Fates
Christmas Travesties
Five Faces of Felicia Clarke
Little Place Called Home
Security Directorate Dossiers v. 1.
Security Directorate Dossiers v. 2.

FICTION
That Love Nonsense
Taipan vs Brown
The Ghost and Ms Cox
Friends Like That
Weaving the Wildwood

MS BLAELOCK'S BOOKS
Stress Free Dinner Parties
Signature Wardrobe Planning
Holistic Personal Finance
Minimally Viable Housekeeping
Planning a Life Worth Living

PICTURE BOOKS
Australia Felix

A SELECTION OF AVAILABLE SHORT STORIES

All In	Honoris Virilis Respectu
Alma's Grace	Mince Pie Mystery
Blood and Bloody Profanity	Remains of Christmas
Cancelled by the Cartel	Shining Star
Dingo Hunting	Susan and the Gangster
Dream House	The Day the Schedule Broke
First Rung	The Trembling Tower

DEVIL YOU DON'T KNOW

A SHORT STORY

ALEXANDRIA BLAELOCK

BlueMere Books
MELBOURNE, AUSTRALIA

For permission requests, please contact enquiries@bluemerebooks.com.

Ordering Information:
Discounts are available on quantity purchases. For details, contact orders@bluemerebooks.com.

Devil You Don't Know /Alexandria Blaelock
paperback ISBN: 9781923083059
digital ISBN: 9781923083066

Book Layout © BookDesignTemplates.com
Cover Art © grandfailure/Depositphotos

Zelda lay still, eyes closed.

Her blind date had turned out to be a real live wire, the life of the party type who would not (or could not) be quiet or still.

And reckless enough to imply he'd taken a not quite legal substance and, therefore, was a danger to himself and others.

More specifically, a danger to her.

Plus, a bit more handsy than she was generally comfortable with on a first date.

Always assuming she liked the guy she was with.

And if he'd tried one more time to get a hand up her Prussian blue, tea-length, silk chiffon layered cocktail dress, she might have been forced to do something regrettable.

She'd managed to get a few steps away while his back was turned.

Then given him the slip by ducking around a corner, dashing a few steps down a kind of short, dark something or other lined corridor, and bolting through an unlocked door into what turned out to be a study or library kind of room.

Not that she was in a position to pick or choose her emergency bolt hole, but it was a pleasant surprise.

The fact of it being a warm, dark, and most importantly, quiet room meant her tense shoulders dropped the minute the heavy door ended the noise and movement with a sharp snick as she swung it shut.

She'd intended to stop for just a moment.

Just enough to give him a little time to wonder where she was and start searching the inner rooms of the mansion for her.

Then she'd planned a midnight flit for freedom. Down the long tree-lined driveway, and out into the street where she could order a cab.

And make a clean getaway.

Stupidly, she'd taken her shoes off and lain down in the dark, on a soft plush, overstuffed *chaise longue* and closed her eyes for a fraction of a second to savour the calm, silent stillness.

Not to mention the smell of lavender and beeswax furniture polish, old books, and a bowl of highly scented homegrown roses somewhere in the room.

And fallen asleep.

She couldn't help it.

She was exhausted after a long and difficult week at work.

The hardest thing about being an Executive Assistant is that your average high-powered executive delegates all the arseholes to you to handle.

Normally Zelda enjoyed dealing with them in such an icily polite manner she almost drew blood.

But now and again you get a week where the moon is just right for them to come out of the woodwork all at once.

And ordinarily, on a Friday night, she'd prefer a dozen or two sojus with Korean fried chicken and an action movie marathon to get over it. Vin Diesel or Jason Statham, maybe even a classic Van Damme

But this weekend, her irritating flatmate had invited her repulsive boyfriend to stay without consultation or notice.

And Zelda was three quarters convinced his "lovemaking" was overly loud and vigorous because he was trying to demonstrate his adequacy as a lover.

To her.

In the vain hope, she'd join in too.

As if!

But she was also a little afraid that one of these nights he'd invite himself into her room if she didn't.

And there are only so many nights you can wedge a chair under the knob of your own bedroom door.

It was probably time to look for a tiny apartment to keep all to herself.

So, she'd agreed to come on this stupid date, to get away from them.

A real frying pan v fire situation the evening had turned out to be.

And so, the study was a welcome island of tranquillity within the noise and clamour of the kind of outrageous party that deserved to be a Hollywood musical all of its own.

Something vintage with Debbie Reynolds in a long ballet pink satin gown and that nice pretty man, what was his name? Donald O'Connor, in a tux.

Except the whispered conversation that woke her up wasn't the kind of sweet whispered conversation you'd get in a Debbie Reynolds movie.

More like a Humphrey Bogart.

Something about thievery and guns and payments.

More like Statham Skulduggery!

And that was why she was lying still and silent, praying to whatever deity might be listening, they wouldn't decide to sit on the *chaise longue* to find she'd got there first.

She concentrated on breathing evenly in the hope that if they discovered her, they would assume she hadn't heard any of it.

For the moment, a deity was with her. With the sound of palms slapping together, they'd reached an agreement and left the room.

And she was left with the troubling decision of how long to give them to get clear before she could leave what was turning out to be the worst date ever.

She remained, eyes closed, still and silent.

Trying to work out where the window was. And whether she could leave the building through it before anyone else walked in. Whether she could get out undetected.

Though this kind of movie, and a lavish party in the house like this, there would be security cameras.

And any kind of non-standard departure was bound to be recorded and investigated.

If the whispering couple were up to something, she'd immediately be a suspect.

Hell, she was probably one already having snuck into the room before them and remaining there after they left.

What, in whatever deity was looking out for her's name, should she do?

Well, seemingly, go right back to sleep.

To be woken by the warm, soft, gentle touch of lips on hers, and going by the spicy cologne, male lips.

Her treacherous body betrayed her with a sigh.

Oh no! What to do now?

"Ah, Sleeping Beauty awakes."

The only thing worse than frying pans and fires was what was happening right now. And as the balance of the *chaise longue* cushions moved, her eyes flicked open to look at him.

He was sitting on the *chaise longue*, very close beside her.

In the warm, dim light of a stained-glass table lamp, she could see he was supporting his body weight with one elbow on the back of the chaise, as he leaned over her. His beautiful, clean-shaven face close enough she could grab his jaw and pull him down for another kiss.

Perhaps a longer, deeper kiss...

And as she looked into his deep brown eyes, partly concealed by the dark fringe of hair falling across his forehead, she was really tempted to.

Because it felt like the world had just contracted to the two of them, alone, in an intimate pool of darkness.

As if this instant was *the* defining moment of her life.

The skin around his eyes crinkled, as if he was smiling, and she guessed he was thinking about kissing too.

Or was hoping.

But much as she wanted it, she knew without a doubt, a second kiss would come with some kind of price. Whether it was her body, her soul, or her mind.

And right now, she just didn't have the strength to deal with anything outside her life as it stood.

She shifted with the intention of sitting up to prevent the kiss, but he was sitting on her skirt, and she couldn't get away without tearing it.

He smoothed his red patterned tie down the front of his shirt, "I guess I've been a *very* good boy if Santa delivered you to my room."

"I apologise," she said, "I had a headache and needed somewhere quiet to rest."

"Then don't mind me, rest some more."

He leaned a little closer, and she thought he *really* was going to kiss her, but he just adjusted the cushions she was resting on instead.

"No really," she tried unsuccessfully to sit up again, "I should go."

"But we've barely got to know each other yet."

Zelda gathered a bunch of skirt material and pulled it out from underneath him with barely a grunt.

Then bent her knees, scooted back up the seat to free her legs, and managed to overbalance onto the floor.

And slid back out of arms reach.

"It's kind of you to offer, but I really must go."

She scrambled to her feet and bolted for the door.

And was halfway down the drive before she realised she'd left her shoes behind.

Her favourite Prussian blue patent Mary Janes. The retro ones with pointy toes, low Cuban heels and a semi-circle of teardrop cut outs around the arch. Oddly, the most comfortable shoes she owned.

On the bright side, she'd reflexively grabbed her evening bag on the way through.

She hopped from bare foot to bare foot for a few seconds before choosing to abandon them and keep running.

Except when she got to the bottom and looked back up to the brightly lit house, party still in full swing, she wondered why she'd run.

Too many romantic comedies probably.

While she waited for the car, the calm of that guy's study lingering on her skin like lotion, she realised she couldn't face going home right then.

Her flatmate, the boyfriend, the noise, the embarrassment, the insecurity.

God her life sucked.

Well, life outside of work anyway.

It wasn't the house, or the man that made the rest of her life suddenly surplus to requirements.

It was that one room, imbued with who knows how many generations of people quietly reading, or writing, or simply going about their business.

She wanted that sense of peacefulness.

Of being in the right place, at the right time, doing the right thing.

She definitely needed to find a new place of her own.

But for the moment, a hotel would do.

She toyed with using the one her company had an agreement with, but its modernity really didn't appeal.

Didn't she get an offer for that swanky new spa hotel in the old treasury building?

She grabbed her phone, opened up her mail app and scrolled through her mail hoping she hadn't deleted the offer.

And found it, it looked good, she rang and booked herself in for the weekend.

Then texted her flatmate to say she wouldn't be back for a couple of days.

The nineteenth-century Renaissance Revival style hotel was an oasis of tranquillity.

Might have been something to do with its long history, or more probably something to do with the pool and fountain in the foyer.

And the discreet staff ignoring her lack of luggage and shoes.

While she waited for them to finish the check-in procedure and give her the welcome spiel about rooms and facilities and treatments, she felt the hair on the back of her neck rise.

She turned to see a dark-haired guy in a dinner suit sitting in a wing backed chair, one leg slung across the other.

He looked vaguely familiar, and she wondered if she'd seen him at the party.

She met his deep brown eyes when he looked at her over the top of the newspaper he was reading.

He looked at her for a while longer, then nodded at her.

She nodded back, fully prepared to enjoy the view a little longer, but the woman behind the check-in desk claimed her attention.

Her room was large, smelled clean and fresh, and had a beautiful view over the gardens. Through a window she opened to let the night air in.

The crisply made bed was enormous.

She took a quick shower, pulled on the white, fluffy bathrobe and slipped her feet into the soft matching slippers.

Being a practical Executive Assistant, she washed out her underwear and hung them in the open wardrobe to dry.

Suddenly realising she'd barely eaten since lunch and was starving, so she ordered soup from room service.

She flicked through the channels looking for something to watch. But after everything else she'd been through that evening, the noise of it was too much to deal with.

So, she sat in the glow of a bedside lamp, drinking her soup, watching the moths dance in and out of the garden lights.

Peaceful. Tranquil. Contented.

She slept deeply, and well, and woke early to the first light of dawn sneaking in the window.

《《 • 》》

The thing about a Prussian blue cocktail dress made from layers of silk chiffon is that it makes you instantly, and unavoidably visible in a sea of black cocktail gowns.

And early morning shoppers, especially when you're striding barefoot along City streets.

Eating a pastry in one hand, clutching an evening bag with the other.

Not exactly *Breakfast at Tiffany's*, but good enough.

Zelda felt she ought to be wand shopping, not clothes shopping. Though she only needed enough to get through the next couple of days.

Wearing her new jeans, t-shirt, sneakers and cardigan out, she carried her dress, new spare t-shirt and undies in a new tote bag. She didn't bother with more makeup but did pick up some skincare.

With something more casual to wear, she stopped at a burger bar for something more substantial to eat. She took a seat in the window and watched people in the street as she ate.

And felt the hair on the back of her neck stand up.

She smoothed it down, and it rose again.

As she popped the last bite in her mouth and wiped her hands with a napkin, she noticed a dark-haired man wearing a white suit standing on the other side of the street.

He looked vaguely familiar, but she didn't think too much about it.

Except, he seemed to be looking at her.

She didn't bother looking behind her because she knew the place was empty.

There wasn't anyone else inside he could be looking at except her.

Assuming he was looking at her, and not at the building.

Or a bird on a window ledge.

Or the car parked out front.

Or anything really.

She wiped her lips, collected her bag, and dumped her rubbish in the bin.

And when she left the restaurant, he was gone.

Seeing as she had no other plans until her mid-afternoon massage back at the hotel, she did some window shopping.

Stopping to idly look at the sale and rental flyers in a real estate office window.

And saw one for a tiny apartment in a Romanesque Gothic Style building near her office. One she loved so much she often took lunchtime walks just to walk past it.

And it was up for rent at a ridiculously low price.

She reached for the handle of the door and saw the white suited burger bar guy reflected in the glass.

She turned to look behind her, but he'd gone.

And when she reached for the door again, she searched the reflection but didn't see him.

But once again, the hair on the back of her neck was rising.

She rolled her head back and forth across her shoulders and went inside to make an appointment to look at the place Monday lunchtime.

《《 • 》》

Zelda guessed Monday was going to be frantic and dressed in her black wool crepe power suit. The one with a long pencil skirt and short fitted jacket that made her feel like a very efficient 1930s secretary.

And as she sat in the train for her hour-long commute, considered how wonderful it might be to take a short stroll into the office from that apartment instead.

Zelda loved the office she worked in, with its marble floors, the enormous flower arrangements, and best of all, the red "Persian" carpet in the Director's waiting area. Not to mention the stunning view over the city, and if she leaned a little, the top of that Romanesque Gothic Style apartment building.

It was, of course, a busy morning dealing with correspondence, scheduling, and collating committee papers. The kid of busy she enjoyed the most.

And she needed the distraction to keep her mind off her appointment to view the apartment.

So, when lunchtime arrived, and it was time to go see the apartment, she was relatively calm.

And waiting in the foyer for the Realtor, she enjoyed examining the ironwork around the entrance, the terrazzo floors, brass fixtures and marble cladding on the interior walls.

Catching a glimpse of herself in the glass window panels, she thought with her vintage style suit and short bobbed hair, she looked a good fit for the place.

Like a vintage ad, with a dark-haired man in a white suit on the stairs, looking longingly at her.

She was so sure he was real and not imaginary, she turned to look, and of course, no one was there.

The third-floor, open plan one-bedroom apartment was glorious. Rich red wood floorboards, adorably tiny ironwork balcony, and beautifully lead lighted windows showcasing expansive views over the nearby park.

The kitchen and bathroom were clean and compact, and the bedroom included well-designed built-in storage with drawers, shelves and hanging space.

Best of all, a large blank corner where she could install bookshelves and go some way towards recreating that study with a *chaise longue* and replica tiffany lamp.

Clean, empty and ready to move in.

Zelda signed the lease swiped her card for the bond and first month's rent and accepted the key.

And thought about getting some new furniture.

Some other day because she was late back to work.

She'd just made it back to her desk when the main reception called to let her know the Director's next appointment had arrived; a Mr Fitzgerald.

She dropped her bag in the bottom drawer of her desk cabinet, and let her boss know she was going to collect him.

During the short elevator ride, she smoothed down her suit and patted her bobbed hair into place.

The dark-haired man in a navy suit had his back to her, hands lightly clasped behind him, looking out the window.

From her vantage point, he was youngish, tall and slim with a little tightness here and there in the fit of his high-end suit that suggested muscles lay beneath. His red tie, reflected in the window back at her, looked askew.

There was something about him that tickled the back of her memory.

"Mr Fitzgerald?"

He turned, and for a moment she couldn't move, shocked into speechlessness.

Was he the guy from the party?

And if, as he claimed, she'd been in his room, that enormous house belonged to him.

And as she watched him walk towards her, her vision blurred, and she thought maybe he was the black suit guy from the hotel. And he was strikingly similar to the white-suited guy she'd seen at the apartment building.

Only better dressed.

Were they triplets?

Or was it possible they were all the same guy?

"Zelda Smith?" he asked.

She nodded, and he held out his hand, "Scott."

One breath of his spicy cologne and she knew it was him.

"Scott?" she asked, "as in Scott Fitzgerald?"

He smiled thinly, "Yes. My parents were fans. And my given name is Francis, but I don't use it."

She tried to stifle it, but the snort came out anyway.

His face hardened.

"I'm sorry. It's just one of those random coincidences, isn't it?"

He raised an eyebrow.

She rolled her eyes, "Zelda and F. Scott Fitzgerald?"

"Oh, I see! Yes. I suppose it is a bit random."

He seemed sensitive about it, so she gestured towards the lift, "if you'll come with me," and left him to his thoughts during the ride.

Having him in her world, so to speak, tipped it on its axis.

She was glad she'd worn her power suit, and not something less structured.

Though he didn't seem to remember her.

Which was a good thing, right?

Concentrating on her work was difficult, so she switched her attention to the conference she was planning and searched venues and suppliers for a while instead.

Squeezing in a sneaky search or two for bits and pieces for her new apartment, because she didn't own any of the furniture in the apartment she shared.

So, in the end, it seemed like no time at all the meeting was over, and it was time to escort Mr Fitzgerald back to the ground floor.

He was quiet in the lift.

But as they stood by the main doors of the building, he smoothed a hand down his red tie, and tilted his head to look at her from the corners of his eyes.

"I believe I might have something of yours Miss Smith."

"Oh?"

"I think you may have left your blue shoes in my house."

"Oh..." she said blushing.

"That's three marriages you owe me."

She took a step back, "I'm sorry?"

He took a step towards her, and ticked them off on his fingers, "I woke Sleeping Beauty with a kiss.

"I searched the kingdom and matched the shoes with Cinderella.

"And now there's Scott and Zelda."

She fought a smile, "that's quite poetic Mr Fitzgerald. I see you can spin a story as well as your namesake."

He took another step towards her, "I think you should meet me for a drink."

She stood her ground, tilting her chin up towards him, "I'm afraid I'll be washing my hair."

He snorted, "how else will you get your shoes back?"

"Ah. Extortion is it?"

He put his hands behind his back and leaned down towards her, "or we could call it a date."

She frowned when she realised her body was leaning towards him.

She'd just get her shoes and be done with him.

"Okay fine," she snapped, "when."

He laughed, "I'll call you," and walked out the door before she could say anything further.

《《 • 》》

After work, Zelda bought a retractable steel tape measure and dropped past her new apartment. She walked up the stairs, to see if she could make it in one go, but found the last flight a little hard going.

She took some quick measurements and wrote a shopping list of things to buy.

Which was pretty much everything, but her list started with a *chaise longue* she could eat, sleep and read on while she got everything else sorted out.

And a kettle.

She walked down the stairs to the ground, following a tall, slim, dark-haired man in a white suit.

He glanced up at her as he turned the corner.

She thought it might have been Scott Fitzgerald, so she sped up, but didn't catch him. And when she reached the street, she looked in both directions but didn't see him.

When Zelda got home, she told her flatmate she was moving out. The girl had a tantrum and demanded she leave immediately.

Zelda knew she should've been annoyed but was too excited about the new apartment.

And while she knew she should've protested being thrown out on the street, was glad the girl hadn't begged her to stay.

From the minute the apartment door had opened in front of her, she hadn't wanted to be anywhere else.

So, while her ex-flatmate watched, and shouted, she packed her things into her suitcase.

And when that was full, a couple of big black garbage bags.

And before too long, she was back on the street. Waiting for a cab to take her back to her empty apartment.

Job done.

Though it was, of course, an empty apartment.

She unpacked her bags, leaving her laptop and the books she'd been able to salvage on the kitchen bench. Stowing her clothes in the bedroom, toiletries and makeup in the bathroom.

Then she left a voice mail for her boss letting him know she wouldn't be in the next day.

And booked herself back into the spa hotel.

She changed into jeans and a t-shirt, packed a small bag of overnight essentials and was on her way.

After checking in, she thought perhaps she deserved a nightcap.

She went through to the dimly lit, wood-panelled, red paisley carpeted bar, and ordered Cognac.

While she waited, she looked around, thinking it looked and felt a little like Scott Fitzgerald's study.

And down at the carpet, thinking a red paisley rug would look nice in her proto-library.

Across the carpet, a dark-haired guy in a black suit sitting at a table nearby.

For a moment, she thought he was Scott Fitzgerald again, then thought he was more like the guy she'd seen in the hotel on the weekend.

When he folded the newspaper so he could hold it in one hand while he took a sip of something that looked like whisky, she could see it wasn't Scott.

The man in front of her seemed a little older, His face was textured by time and weather. A little white threaded through his hair.

Just someone who looked a lot like Scott.

Only maybe a little sexier.

She sat at the bar, swivelling idly on the barstool, watching people passing in and out of the hotel foyer.

Trying not to think about Scott.

Or anything at all.

"You look different with shoes," his voice was deep and resonant. Weirdly his timbre was ideally suited to the close confines of the small bar.

And she thought perhaps there was some similarity with Scott's tone, phrasing and pacing.

"I'm sorry?"

"I said you look different with shoes."

"Oh, I see. You were here when I checked in on the weekend?"

"Yes.

"Seeing as it's just us, would you care to join me?"

Her brain said shut it down, but some long-hidden streak of wild recklessness stirred within her, so Zelda picked up her drink and took the seat opposite him.

And watched as he refolded the newspaper and leaned over to drop it on the table.

She thought she smelled a familiar spicy scent.

"I feel like I ought to ask if you come here often," she said.

He snorted, his deep brown eyes meeting hers, "actually I do."

"Business?"

"Of course."

Zelda swirled the Cognac in her glass, and inhaled before taking a sip, "you remind me of someone."

"Do I?"

"Yes, a Scott Fitzgerald. Might you be related?"

He grinned as if she'd told a huge joke, "I know of him."

"And?"

"He seems... Stable and dependable."

"You're not really selling him."

"He's young. I'm sure at some point he'll grow into a reliable man."

Zelda wasn't entirely sure what it was she was hoping to find out, or whether this man was deliberately cryptic.

Or whether she could trust anything a stranger said.

But that streak of recklessness rolled over.

"Would you say he was worth my time?"

He sat back in his chair and regarded her steadily.

His gaze was quite direct, taking in her eyes, lips and breasts. Getting beneath her skin, perhaps as deep as her soul.

Strangely exciting.

When he broke it off to pick up his drink, she felt she'd passed some sort of test.

Though she wasn't sure what kind.

"Only you can decide that Cinderella, but you'll never know unless you try."

He drained his drink, "I'll bid you goodnight," then walked out of the bar.

She watched him leave, trying to decide whether to chase after him.

Not entirely sure whether to demand more information about Scott, or whether to suggest she join him in his room.

But given she saw Scott Fitzgerald everywhere, entirely sure this Scott mess was already completely out of control.

《《 • 》》

After a hearty breakfast buffet, Zelda caught a cab to a factory outlet mall in the suburbs.

It seemed Tuesday was her lucky day, as she was able to get the furniture and homewares she needed. And by paying express rates, could get most of it delivered during the afternoon and evening.

Not only that, but she'd barely had to compromise on taste to get what she'd wanted.

How many fairy godmothers, she wondered, did she actually have?

Then another quick lap of the mall for groceries, a bunch of flowers, and other necessities to use before the main deliveries arrived.

And because she was feeling lucky, a couple of scratch lottery tickets too.

Followed by a mid-morning cab ride back to her new home.

She opened the windows to let some fresh air in, gave the kitchen and bathroom a quick clean, put her shopping away, and was ready to receive deliveries with an hour or so to spare.

To fill in the time, she went to the basement to see the surprisingly modern shared laundry.

Then up to the roof to see the common garden.

In the centre, a wood pergola shaded wooden benches arranged in a circle underneath it. Raised beds of shrubs guarded the walls and broke the force of the wind over the roof. Small, bright flowers poked through the lush green leaves. Larger pots of topiary and wild plants created a spiral labyrinth.

Zelda took a deep breath of wild, plant scented air, and turned her face to the sun. She let herself believe for a moment, that there really was some kind of supernatural creature looking out for her.

Her skin prickled.

She opened her eyes and saw a slim dark-haired man in a white suit seated under the pergola. Leaning back, eyes closed, enjoying the sunshine.

Had he been there before, and she hadn't noticed him?

She glanced at her watch, and even though the time frame was getting close, decided to approach him.

"May I join you?"

He opened his eyelids, and his deep brown eyes focused on her for a moment before looking away.

He quickly looked away, patting his pockets as if looking for his phone or keys, "I, uh..."

His movement sent a whiff of a familiar spicy cologne in her direction.

She narrowed her eyes and looked at him more closely.

Slim build, brown eyes, somewhat dark hair, spicy cologne.

The other Scott Fitzgerald clone. The one from the burger bar and real estate office.

He seemed a little too wild and agitated.

"I'm sorry," she said, "I didn't mean to disturb you. I'll leave you to it."

She backed away, then turned and escaped into the building.

Just in time to take her first delivery.

And after that, she on the go for the rest of the day.

Accepting deliveries.

Rushing downstairs to wash her new bed linen and towels. And back down to swap them into the dryer. And back down to bring up her clean and dry washing.

Accepting more deliveries.

Putting load upon load of new cookware, cutlery and dishes in the dishwasher.

Finding homes for the bits and pieces.

Rushing out for a quick bowl of noodle soup, stopping by a bottle shop on the way back for a bottle of champagne.

Accepting the last delivery.

And finally, after a long, hot shower, sitting back, in her clean and furnished apartment.

In front of the tv, with a glass of champagne, enjoying a well-earned break.

《《 • 》》

The next morning, she woke disoriented.

But after going back to sleep again, she woke with a start, realising it was Wednesday, and she should be at work.

And that she had a meeting to minute.

Though luckily, she now lived a short walk from work.

So, after a leisurely shower, and a quick stop to buy coffee and a sweet pastry, she arrived with enough time to prepare for the meeting.

The joy of that was enough to get her through its' tediousness.

For lunch, she picked at a salad at her desk while she checked her voice mail and caught up on her email.

Among which was a message from Scott Fitzgerald suggesting they meet that night.

She couldn't exactly specify why but was inclined to reject him.

Their Monday meeting seemed like a hundred years ago, and the attraction she'd felt for him was diminished. He was still fascinating but seemed ridiculously like a long-lost lover.

Though there were her favourite shoes to consider.

As she thought about it, or maybe him, she wondered if she'd met three Scotts.

Scott with the red tie at the party and office.

Scott in the black suit at the hotel.

Scott in white from the apartment and City.

Not that she knew they were all named Scott.

But they all had a similar slim yet muscular build, dark hair, brown eyes, and wore the same spicy cologne.

And all three made the hair on the back of her neck stand up. Maybe that's why she felt they were the same.

Was there a male equivalent of the triune goddess?

Boy, father, and nut job? Geezer?

What was that party game?

Kiss, marry, kill.

She remembered the first time she'd met Scott at the party, how she'd thought if she kissed him again, it would cost her.

Body, soul, or mind she'd thought.

She set her salad aside and grabbed a pencil and her notebook to work it out.

There was Scott with the red tie at the party and again at her office. The first, the Boy.

Then Scott in the black suits at the hotel (three times). He seemed a little, well not older per se, but experienced. Scott the Father then.

Then Scott in white linen at her apartment building Twice? Three times? And all around the city? Like a crazy stalker version, so, Scott the Geezer.

The Father suggested the Boy might be worth her time. The Boy had kissed her, so was his price her body, and the Father her soul?

The Geezer on the roof had seemed completely freaked out when she'd approached him. What might that say about the Boy? And if she kissed the Boy, and married the Father, did she have to kill the Geezer?

The Boy had referred to three marriages - Sleeping Beauty, Cinderella and the writing Fitzgeralds.

Sleeping Beauty woken by a prince's kiss (or rape if you believe the old tales), she marries him, and allegedly lives happily ever after. It seemed an immature, boyish act.

Cinderella loses a shoe, is sought out by a prince who is fascinated by her, marries him, and lives happily ever after. Or if not happily, then at least comfortably. A deal, perhaps with the devil, costing a soul.

Zelda meets F. Scott at a party. She doubts him, he writes a bestseller, she marries him. She has a mental breakdown, he dies of a heart attack, and she dies in a hospital fire. A relationship destined to go bad and end in an ugly death.

And of those three scenarios, the one most appealing was the one she thought offered her the best odds. Cinderella - Charming at least put some effort into the relationship. Turned the country upside down, rejecting every woman who threw herself at him. That didn't seem likely, but if he hadn't, then at least he had been discrete.

If she had a choice, she wanted Cinderella's prince.

Would that be the man she'd met at the spa hotel then?

She didn't return Scott's call. She diverted her phone to voice mail and focused on getting the minutes typed up and in the mail.

But her thoughts kept returning to the dark-suited man in the hotel.

《《 • 》》

Zelda knew it was reckless, but six-thirty found her in a red cocktail dress, at the bar of the hotel.

She was nervous, she didn't know if the Father, as she'd started thinking of him, was in town.

Let alone whether she'd see him. Or would be eating a light meal of bar snacks before falling back to her apartment to lick her wounds.

He'd said he travelled after all.

And more to the point, she didn't know what the hell she thought she might achieve.

Kiss, marry, kill.

Because he'd said he travelled, and by inference, she'd be on her own. Or maybe travel with him?

Nonetheless, she ordered a Dubonnet cocktail and waited.

Not entirely sure what she was waiting for.

Or what she wanted.

Or how long she should wait for it.

She sat at the table they'd shared a hundred years ago on Monday. Her right leg crossed over her left, left hand resting in her lap, right elbow balancing on her right knee as she held the glass to her lips, the fumes going to her head before she took her first sip.

Feeling once again like a vintage ad. Only this time, with a black-suited man walking across the lobby towards her.

Her heart skipped a beat as the hair on the back of her neck rose.

He came to a stop before her, leaning his weight on one leg, resting a hand on the back of the chair.

His brown eyes and spicy cologne reached out towards her.

"I like this look on you Cinderella."

"Why thank you Charming," she said, "would you care to join me?"

"I'll get a drink, can I get you another?"

"I'm fine."

He boldly met her gaze, "yes, you are."

He returned not much later with an extra Dubonnet for her anyway.

He set the drinks on the table and took the seat next to her.

"How did you know what to get?"

He smiled and shrugged one shoulder, "asked the bartender for another of whatever you had before. What is it?"

She smiled in return, "Dubonnet cocktail, want a taste?"

He met her eyes as he took the glass from her hand and raised it to his lips, "bittersweet."

He handed it back.

She smiled slightly, "life's but a walking shadow. A poor player that struts and frets his hour upon the stage, and then is heard no more."

"Shakespeare?"

She nodded and put her glass down, "*Macbeth*."

"A tragic tale for so early in the evening."

She shrugged, "perhaps, but in the end, life is often tragic."

He grunted noncommittally and took a sip of his drink.

"What are you drinking?"

"Whisky."

He held the glass out toward her but didn't let it go as she reached out for it.

His hand was hot beneath hers.

He leaned forward, guiding the glass to her lips, tilting it just enough for a little to burn her lips as the whisky passed through them.

She held it in her mouth, considering the complexity of the taste and what it told her about him. Smoke, leather, wood, tobacco.

Straightforward.

Unambiguous.

Direct.

She swallowed and watched him sip from the glass.

"Unmistakable."

He laughed and nudged her knee with his, "a better word than obvious."

She was tempted to steal another sip from his glass but settled for throwing back what was left of her first cocktail and placing the empty glass on the table with barely a sound.

She reached for the drink he'd bought and took a sip.

Though she hadn't eaten much, and the first drink had definitely gone to her head.

Reckless.

"I'm Zelda."

"I know."

"You know? How do you know?"

He picked her empty hand from the chair arm and wrapped it in his.

"I've been following you for a while."

"Following? Oh, you mean social media?"

"Not exactly. But I found there's no one else like you."

She snorted.

"No, it's true. I've searched all the universes, and there isn't another Zelda anywhere."

"*All* the universes?"

"All of them."

She took a sip of her drink and screwed up her face as she thought about it. "Okay, let's say there are other universes, and you've travelled them all, are you like Dr Who?"

"Doctor who?"

"Exactly, Dr Who."

"I don't know who that is."

"He's like a time traveller, and he gets inside a Police Box and travels across space and time."

"Really?"

"Are you dumb? It's a tv show."

"Ah. Okay," he paused for a moment while he thought about it, lazily stroking the back of her hand with his thumb. "I guess I kind of am a bit like Dr Who. Only I don't have a machine, I just walk through doors."

"Doors? What kind of story is that? If you're travelling to other universes, you should be travelling through carved granite gateways in a fizz of fluorescent coloured light."

He looked at her blankly.

"Okay, that's *Star Trek*. Wait, how do you not know about *Star Trek*?

No, that's not the point. The nub of the matter I'm trying to get to, is if you're an immortal creature from another planet?"

"No."

"Or some kind of supernatural creature with paranormal abilities?"

"No."

"Human?"

"Most decidedly."

"Right," she took another sip of her drink, "just crazy then."

"Absolutely not." He turned his head to look at her, eyes twinkling, lips twitching, "want me to show you?"

"Maybe, but first you must tell me your name."

"Didn't I tell you? I'm Scott Fitzgerald?"

She snorted, "next you'll be claiming to be the original and best."

"I don't need to. You're here with me, not that other pale imitation."

"Argh! Outdone by my own logic."

"So, shall I rock your universe?"

Zelda turned her face towards him, trying to reading his. It was alive with mischief, and for a second or two, she believed he didn't need a stone portal because he was the flicker of fluorescent coloured light that made it all work.

And then she blinked and told herself he just wanted to have sex with her.

So, she drained the second cocktail and stood up.

He smiled, and she caught her breath, thinking she'd seen triumph in his face.

But if it had been there at all, it was soon gone.

He squeezed her hand and started walking towards the hotel lift.

After pushing the button for his floor, he grabbed her other hand and pulled her so close their bodies touched.

She gasped.

He wrapped her arms around him and leaned down to kiss her.

She didn't notice when the lift chimed their arrival, or the doors opened.

And followed him blindly towards a door at the end of the corridor.

He pulled an unexpectedly ornate key from his breast pocket and inserted it into the lock.

She paused, wondering why he had an actual metal key and not a key card.

And why the door didn't seem to have a card reader.

He leaned on the door frame, blocking her path.

"If you follow me through this door, there's no coming back."

She snorted, "yeah right, the door will disappear?"

"It's true. There's only one of you, there's no one to hold your place if you leave."

"Scott, do you have much success with this chat-up line?"

"I don't usually bother to warn anyone."

She shook her head and turned to walk away, "honestly, you can't be that good in bed."

But he grabbed her hand, "don't leave me, I've come a long way for you."

"Then open the goddamned door, and let's get on with it."

On the other side of the door, was a perfectly ordinary hotel room, a lot like the one she'd stayed in over the weekend.

She took a step forward.

Reckless.

He put out his arm to bar her path, "wait! Are you sure?"

She put her direct her hips and rolled her eyes.

He stepped back into the room, and the lights flickered.

She stepped over the threshold and felt a slight zing of electricity.

He kissed her, then picked her up and carried her to the bed.

《《 • 》》

Zelda smiled and stretched.

He'd been an enthusiastic and energetic lover, but now she was starving and wanted breakfast.

She crawled out of bed, slapping his hands out of the way before he could stop her.

After a visit to the bathroom, she went to open the curtains so she could check the room service menu for breakfast.

"Wait," he cried, but it was too late.

For a moment, it looked like an ordinary day. Blue skies, mid-morning sunshine. Hot air balloons bobbing above a cityscape that wasn't quite right.

She couldn't quite pinpoint what was wrong about it and turned to look at Scott, who was shielding his eyes from the brightness.

She looked again and tried to pick out the buildings she knew. No sign of the Parliament, the Exchange building or the hotel gardens.

She scrubbed her eyes and looked again.

Scott walked behind her and wrapped his arms around her, pulling her back to lean against his chest.

He kissed the top of her head, "I told you."

"Yeah, but I thought you were just talking up your sexual prowess."

He squeezed her, "and did I meet your expectations?"

She reached behind him to pat his bottom, "you weren't bad."

"Another round?"

Zelda was conflicted.

She was hungry.

If he was telling the truth, and the view from the window suggested he was, she'd just lost everything she knew to be true.

But...

If he'd searched all the universes for her. That was an extraordinary level of determination to find the one woman who fit the shoes.

Bittersweet.

"Do you have Cinderella's shoes?"

"What?"

"My blue shoes? The ones that started all this?"

He scuffed a toe on the carpet, and she imagined he looked sheepish.

She rotated her head but couldn't see the expression on his face.

He let her go and opened the wardrobe to reveal a pair of blue shoes.

They were the right shoes, but like the view from the window, not quite right.

Still, it was enough.

Plus, he knew what he was doing in the bedroom.

"Tomorrow, and tomorrow, and tomorrow," she said.

Macbeth again.

Be careful what you wish for, because you just might get it.

THE END

ABOUT THE AUTHOR

Alexandria Blaelock writes stories, some of them for *Ellery Queen's Mystery Magazine* and *Pulphouse Fiction Magazine*.

She's also written five self-help books applying business techniques to personal matters like getting dressed, cleaning house, and feeding your friends.

Discover more at www.alexandriablaelock.com.

www.ingramcontent.com/pod-product-compliance
Lightning Source LLC
Chambersburg PA
CBHW031258210726
48287CB00003B/1078